D0525461

The Night-Time Knight

Also by John McLay and Martin Brown:
The Dragon's Dentist
The Worst Wizard

There are lots of Early Reader stories
you might enjoy.
For a complete list, visit
www.orionchildrensbooks.co.uk

The Night-Time Knight

By John McLay

Illustrated by Martin Brown

Orion
Children's Books

First published in Great Britain in 2016
by Hodder and Stoughton

1 3 5 7 9 10 8 6 4 2

Text copyright © John McLay, 2016
Illustrations copyright © Martin Brown, 2016

The moral rights of the author and illustrator have been asserted.

All characters and events in this publication, other than those clearly
in the public domain, are fictitious and any resemblance to
real persons, living or dead, is purely coincidental.

All rights reserved.
No part of this publication may be reproduced, stored in
a retrieval system, or transmitted, in any form or by any means,
without the prior permission in writing of the publisher, nor be
otherwise circulated in any form of binding or cover other than that
in which it is published and without a similar condition including this
condition being imposed on the subsequent purchaser.

A CIP catalogue record for this book
is available from the British Library.

ISBN 978 1 4440 1292 7

Printed and bound in China

The paper and board used in this book are from well-managed forests
and other responsible sources.

Orion Children's Books
An imprint of Hachette Children's Group
Part of Hodder and Stoughton
Carmelite House
50 Victoria Embankment
London EC4Y 0DZ

An Hachette UK Company
www.hachette.co.uk
www.hachettechildrens.co.uk

To George

Contents

Chapter One

Harry is a famous knight.

He's tall and brave in battle.

Dragons fear him.

Giants run when they see him
coming.

Harry's horse is the biggest and
bravest horse in all the kingdom.

Other knights think Harry is the boldest knight since knights were invented. Which was a very long time ago.

Harry also dreams a lot.
In real life, he cleans shields.
Dirty ones.

He's small and is only a
knight-in-waiting.

His horse, Oats, is a chunky
pony who likes eating oats.
Loads of them.

"My name might be at the top
of the list to become the next
knight," said Harry. "But it's
taking ages."
"Hurry up!" he shouted into
the night.

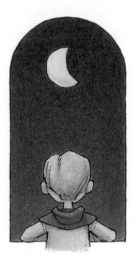

Chapter Two

One morning, Harry was having his breakfast with Oats and his knightly family.

On the long castle table was a simple meal of oats in milk, oat flapjacks, oat bread and some oat sticks.

His brother and sister were eating and arguing about who had the sharpest sword.

His dad was eating and polishing his helmet.

His mum was eating and
knitting some chainmail.

Everyone was ignoring Harry
as he fed oats to Oats.

"Did anybody hear those strange noises coming from the dungeons last night?" said Harry's mum.

"I was fast asleep," said his dad.
"I was tired after that big battle
yesterday."

"Not me," said Harry's brother.
"All that sword practice yesterday
wore me out."

"Me neither," said his sister.
"I needed my beauty sleep."

"I'm sure it was nothing," said Harry's mum. "It did sound quite awful, though." She went back to her chainmail knitting.

Harry and Oats looked at each other.

Harry wondered if there was a mystery to solve. He had to prove himself worthy of being a knight like the rest of his family.

He smelled adventure.

Chapter Three

That night, Harry and Oats tried
to stay awake to see if they could
hear the strange noise, too. It was
very hard.

Suddenly, in the middle of the night, Harry and Oats were woken up by weird sounds.

Lots of weird sounds.

It was a sort of scratching and a
loud scraping.

Then there were crashes and
bangs. And a few moans.

Harry was surprised that the whole
castle was not awake by now.

"Let's go and investigate, Oats. This could be our chance to be knightly!"

Harry put on his helmet and grabbed his dragon-tooth sword.

He led Oats down some winding steps towards the castle dungeons. He knew he had to be brave. Just like a real knight.

Oats put on his bravest long face. He was not sure about this adventure at all.

Chapter Four

Harry and Oats crept through
the creepy castle dungeons. They
were gloomy and smelly and there
were cobwebs everywhere.

As they tiptoed, the strange
noises were getting louder.
Then Harry spotted some ghostly
shadows on a wall.

Something, or someone, was
around the next corner.

The shadows were getting bigger.
Harry held his breath and closed
one eye.

He gripped his sword tightly.

Oats fainted.

From around the corner came ...
a girl.

The girl was carrying a candle,
smelling the air and banging the
walls as she walked.

She stopped in front of Harry
and Oats.
"Oh. Hello," she said.
"Who are you?"

Harry was glad that she wasn't
a hungry monster, deep in the
dungeon.

"Hello," he said. "I'm Harry and this is Oats. We live here."
"Oh," said the girl.

Nobody spoke. It was a little bit awkward.

"So," said Harry, at last. "What's your name? And why are you creeping around our castle in the middle of the night?"

The girl looked sheepish. "I can explain."

She tapped on the wall again. Then sniffed it. "My name is Kestrel," she said, "and I'm looking for treasure!"

Chapter Five

Oats' ears pricked up. Harry's eyes
went wide.

"Treasure? Really? Are you sure?"
Harry looked at Oats. "Do any
of the other horses know about
hidden treasure, Oats?"

Oats shook his head.

"It's true," said Kestrel. "My father says so. He is a great wizard and everything he says is true."

"Is your dad called Hocus Pocus?" said Harry. "The weird wizard who gave me this helmet but who really isn't very good at spells."

"**No,**" said Kestrel.

"Is he called Eric? And does he like planting knights in his garden?"

"**No,**" said Kestrel.

Harry thought again. "Is your dad Merlin? The legend that has been helping kings rule for a thousand years?"

"Yes!" said Kestrel.

"And he's lost his treasure. His magical treasure. It's here somewhere – because I've smelled it."

"Magic smells?" said Harry.

"It sure does." She took a big deep breath. "It pongs down here and I think that's magic."

Harry rubbed his chin. "OK, then. We'll help you. Let's go and find that treasure!"

Chapter Six

"Wait a minute," said Kestrel, as they went deeper underground. "I've been looking down here for days for Merlin's magic mountain of treasure. What makes you think you can find it?"

Harry smiled. He looked at Oats.
"I won't," he said. "Oats will."
Kestrel looked confused.

"That smell has a whiff of
something oaty about it," said
Harry. "I think it may be coming
from the winter oats store. And my
horse is brilliant at finding oats."

Several corners later they came to a big door.

Behind the door was a mountain of oats in bags and barrels and buckets.

Behind the oats was another door.
They pushed it open.
Inside a small room was a heap
of trinkets and spell books and
strange glowing objects that
looked . . . magical.

"Hoorah! We've found it!" said
Kestrel.
Harry patted Oats. "Well done,
old boy."

"Father will be pleased," said Kestrel.
"He'll want you to have something
as a reward for finding it."
Harry looked around at all the
treasure. "Really?"

Oats nudged a shield lying
half-hidden on the floor next
to a pile of books.

"I think I'll take this shield," said
Harry, beaming. "Is it magic?"
"Probably," said Kestrel, smiling.

At breakfast next morning, Harry's brother spied his new shield. "Nice shield, squirt," he said. "Where did you get it from?"

Harry polished it with his sleeve. "Merlin's daughter gave it to me for helping her find a huge pile of treasure under the castle." Harry's sister laughed. "Yeah, right. At least you won't need to borrow mine any more."

"No," said Harry, smiling. "With my sword, helmet and new shield I've now got everything I need to be a knight!"